The Town Mouse and the Country Mouse

Illustrated by Jacqueline East

Retold by Susanna Davidson
Based on a story by Aesop

In among the waving grasses,

lies a little brown country mouse, fast asleep.
His name is Pipin.

He dreams of crunchy seeds
and juicy red strawberries.

Every evening Pipin
pattered home...

...to his little house
in the leafy hedge.

Until, one cold winter's day, there was
a RAT-A-TAT-TAT at his door.

"Pipin!" cried a voice.
It was Toby Town Mouse, come to stay.

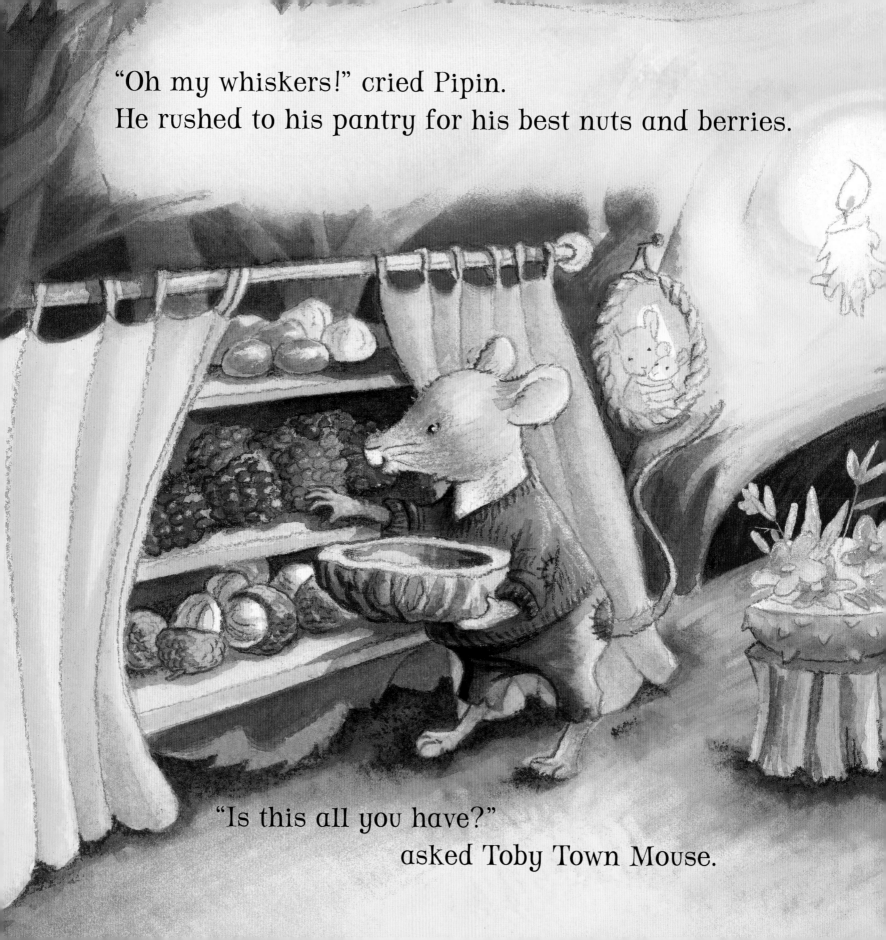

"Oh my whiskers!" cried Pipin.
He rushed to his pantry for his best nuts and berries.

"Is this all you have?"
asked Toby Town Mouse.

"In town we eat like kings.
I think you'd better come and stay with me."

The mice scampered to the station
early next morning.

The train trundled in with
a snort and a shriek.

"It's HUGE!" gasped Pipin.
"It's like a **big**
red
beast."

They wriggled inside a man's
green bag and were lifted aboard. Then...

Chugga-chugga-chugga. Choo! Choo!
They were off!

Pipin gazed out of the window,
at trees waving their branches.

Then there were no trees at all –
just tall buildings that touched the sky.

"At last!" cried Toby, sniffing the air. "We're here!"

Hurry up, Pipin!

They ran out of the station onto a busy street.

"Help!" squeaked Pipin, dodging in and out of stamping feet.

"This is it," said Toby, proudly pointing his paw. "My house."
They crept through a crack under the blue front door.

Toby led Pipin down under the floor,
up secret stairs behind the walls

and into a splendid dining hall.

The mice nibbled
and gnawed

and scooped cream
with their paws,

until they were
perfectly full.

They woke with a start as the table shook.

"MY dinner time!"
purred the kitchen cat.

"Run!" squeaked Toby.

The mice darted
this way
and that.

Pounce! Pounce!
went the hungry cat.

She swiped at Pipin
with her pointy claws.

Quick, Pipin! Into this hole.

Pipin ran.

The cat leaped...

...and missed.
"Curses!" she hissed.

"Oh my whiskers," said Pipin, mopping his brow.
"I want to go home."

Oh! Why?

"This town life is too much for me."

Toby took Pipin to the station
and waved goodbye.

Pipin gazed again
as tall buildings
flashed quickly
past his eyes.

In the starry dark, Pipin
finally reached his hedge.

He sniffed the cold, sweet air and smiled.

Then he snuggled down
in his soft, mossy bed.

"This is the life for me," he said.

Edited by Jenny Tyler and Lesley Sims

Designed by Caroline Spatz

Digital manipulation by John Russell

First published in 2007 by Usborne Publishing Ltd, 83-85 Saffron Hill, London EC1N 8RT, England.
www.usborne.com Copyright © 2007 Usborne Publishing Ltd. The name Usborne and the devices ♀ ⊕ are Trade Marks
of Usborne Publishing Ltd. All rights reserved. No part of this publication may be reproduced, stored in a retrieval system,
or transmitted in any form or by any means, electronic, mechanical, photocopying, recording or otherwise,
without the prior permission of the publisher. First published in America in 2007. UE. Printed in Dubai.